KELE'S SECRET

KELE'S SECRET

by **TOLOLWA M. MOLLEL**

illustrated by
CATHERINE STOCK

LODESTAR BOOKS
Dutton   New York

in memory of
my grandmother, Natoiwoki Mungaya—T.M.M.

for Rosalina Mapyane—C.S.

Text copyright © 1997 by Tololwa M. Mollel
Illustrations copyright © 1997 by Catherine Stock

Library of Congress Cataloging-in-Publication Data
Mollel, Tololwa M. (Tololwa Marti)
   Kele's secret / by Tololwa M. Mollel ; illustrated by Catherine Stock.
        p.   cm.
      "Lodestar books."
      Summary: A young African boy who lives with his grandparents
on their coffee farm follows their hen in order to find out where
she is hiding her eggs.
      ISBN 0-525-67500-0 (alk. paper)
      [1. Chickens—Fiction.   2. Grandparents—Fiction.   3. Tanzania—Fiction.]
   I. Stock, Catherine, ill.   II. Title.
   PZ7.M7335Ke   1997
   [E]—dc20   95-43576
                                                            CIP
                                                            AC

Published in the United States by Lodestar Books,
an affiliate of Dutton Children's Books,
a division of Penguin Books USA Inc.,
375 Hudson Street, New York, New York 10014

Published simultaneously in Canada
by Stoddart Publishing Co., Limited,
Toronto, Canada

Editor: Rosemary Brosnan Designer: Christy Hale
Printed in Hong Kong First Edition 10 9 8 7 6 5 4 3 2 1

Grandmother Koko's hens laid their eggs in the strangest places.

One egg I found in the dark, cluttered loft of Grandfather
Akwi's bedroom.

Another was in the gloomy cow barn on straw brought in for a sleeping calf.

I came upon one more in a spidery corner of the outhouse near Akwi's coffee farm.

Yet another lay on a cushion of leaves deep in a cluster of gnarled bamboo roots and stems.

Carefully . . . I placed all the day's eggs into a gigantic checkered bowl in Grandmother Koko's bedroom.

Koko smiled. "When the bowl is full, Yoanes, we'll take the eggs to the market, you and I."

I thought of the reward Koko gave me whenever I helped her with market work, and I smiled back. "Yes, Koko!"

Then I wished the bowl were full already.

In the evening, Koko told me, "Kele has started laying eggs but is keeping it a real secret. Find out where she lays them."

Kele was Koko's most unusual hen. She looked just like a type of wild fowl called *enkelesurre*. We named her after the bird.

I hardly slept that night. I was so excited I couldn't wait for daylight to find out Kele's secret. Her eggs would help me fill the bowl.

Next morning, I kept a careful watch on Kele. I trailed her as she searched for food—inside houses, in the dust, in the mud, on the grass, and all around the compound.

Soon she made her way to Akwi's coffee farm,
and I followed.

The dense, jungly coffee bushes and the trees on
the farm swallowed up the sun above me. Kele stopped
to scratch and peck at the ground. Then she moved off.

When she came to an old avocado tree, she suddenly
jumped and clucked in panic. Had she seen me? I huddled
behind a tree stump. We both listened to a woodpecker's
furious *tap-tap-tap* on the avocado tree.

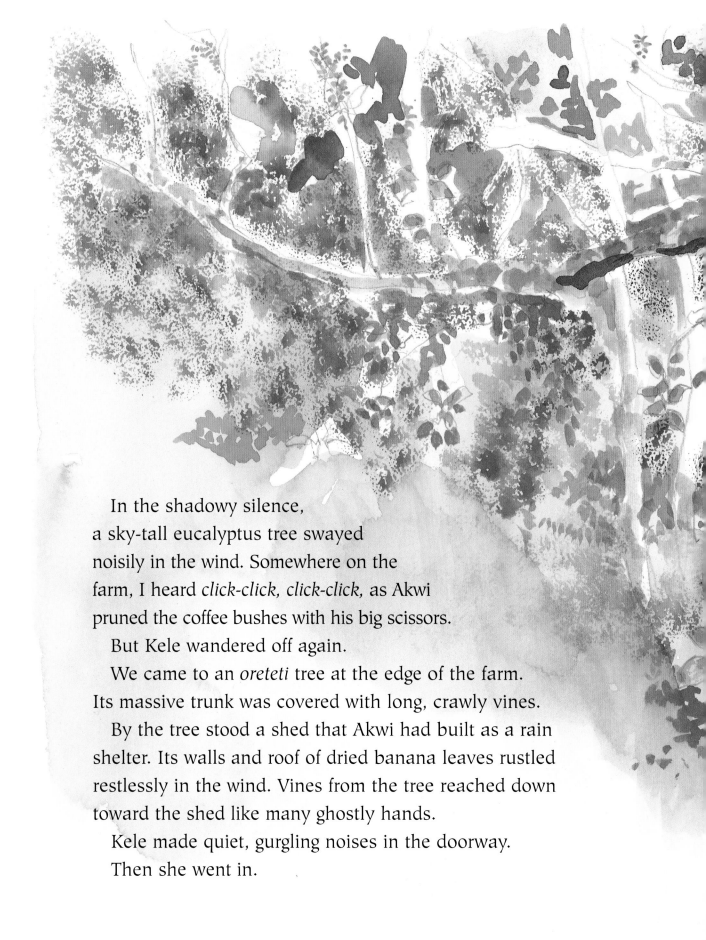

In the shadowy silence,
a sky-tall eucalyptus tree swayed
noisily in the wind. Somewhere on the
farm, I heard *click-click, click-click,* as Akwi
pruned the coffee bushes with his big scissors.

But Kele wandered off again.

We came to an *oreteti* tree at the edge of the farm.
Its massive trunk was covered with long, crawly vines.

By the tree stood a shed that Akwi had built as a rain
shelter. Its walls and roof of dried banana leaves rustled
restlessly in the wind. Vines from the tree reached down
toward the shed like many ghostly hands.

Kele made quiet, gurgling noises in the doorway.

Then she went in.

I stared uneasily into the cavelike shed.

I wasn't afraid to clamber into Akwi's dark, cluttered loft. I wasn't afraid of the gloomy cow barn. I wasn't afraid of the spidery corners of the outhouse. I wasn't afraid to go in deep among the bamboo.

But I had never gone into the creepy shed alone! I listened to the *thump-thump* of my heart and imagined the sound of Nenauner, a half-human, half-rock monster in Koko's bedtime stories. His stone leg drummed the earth as he came toward me from the shed; his robe of dried banana leaves flapped about.

All at once, I heard a screech. Wings aflutter, Kele
came streaking out of the shed, followed by a bat.
The bat scraped against my cheek.

I screamed.

I fell to the ground, too terrified to move. With my
heart pounding, I braced myself to meet Nenauner.
But no one came out of the shed. I watched and waited.
Akwi's scissors had stopped their *click-click*. Away in town,
a car honked *teee-teeeet*. I heard people cheer wildly at a
soccer game in the big stadium by the market.

Suddenly I wished I could go to the market soon.

I crept slowly forward.

I hesitated at the doorway. My eyes darted around the shed, which grew brighter as I got used to the dark. My heart calmed down. There *wasn't* anyone in the shed.

A few steps inside, I stopped.

Lying there, like a gathering of white hills at dawn, were a dozen or so eggs in a corner of the shed, all different shapes, sizes, and shades.

Just then, a shadow darkened the shed. I jumped. "Look at that!" Akwi remarked, gazing down at the eggs beside me. He smiled mischievously. "I was watching and wondering what you were up to."

With Akwi's floppy hat, I brought the eggs safely home.
"Good heavens, Yoanes!" Koko cried in amazement.

Excitedly I told her of my journey after Kele and *into* the
shed. Koko thanked me over and over for the eggs. "Lucky
thing you found them before some greedy snake did!"

I felt like quite a hero when Akwi nodded in agreement.

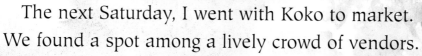

The next Saturday, I went with Koko to market.
We found a spot among a lively crowd of vendors.

By noon, Koko had sold everything—the beans,
bananas, sweet potatoes, *nyafu,* avocados, and dozens
of eggs. She gave me ten cents for helping, a thick red
coin with a hole in the middle. "Buy yourself something.
Anything you want."

"Thank you, Koko!" I said and headed toward a
delicious-looking spread of rice cakes, *mandasi,* dates,
roasted peanuts, and fried cassava and fish.

That night, Kele settled down to warm some of her eggs, which Koko had set aside for hatching. She sat in Koko's bedroom, in the special place we had prepared. Watching Kele in the dim light of a kerosene lamp, I imagined bowls and bowls of eggs and days and days of going to the market, Koko and I.

Kele closed her eyes in sleep.

Quietly Koko picked up the kerosene lamp, and I followed her softly to the kitchen for supper.

AUTHOR'S NOTE

Like Yoanes in the story, I, too, lived with my grandparents on a coffee farm, together with numerous other grandchildren, in the East African country of Tanzania. We all helped with the work. We did chores galore—house chores for Grandmother, farm chores for Grandfather.

With all those children to look after, Grandmother had to be quite a manager. She maintained her sanity by assigning everyone a task, keeping us too busy to cause much trouble. She had a strong, silent authority. Grandmother hardly ever needed to yell to get things done. A look or word was enough. Not that we minded doing our chores—well, not *all* the time.

The story has a few words in Arusha Maasai, one of at least 130 ethnic languages in Tanzania that co-exist with the official national language, Kiswahili.

GLOSSARY

Akwi (ah QUEE)   grandfather or old man

enkelesurre (ehn keh leh SOO reh)   a wild fowl

Kele (Keh LEH)

Koko (KOH koh)   grandmother or old woman

mandasi (mahn DAH see)   deep-fried buns that taste almost like doughnuts

Nenauner (neh NOW nehrr)   a half-human, half-rock creature in Arusha Maasai folklore

nyafu (nyah PHOO)   wild, bitter spinach

oreteti (oh reh teh TEE)   a massive type of vine-covered fig tree believed by some Arusha Maasai to be the abode of ancestral spirits